WANTED
THE DIRTY ROTTEN DOZEN
COOKED OR ALIVE

BENEDICT BENNY

POACHED PETEY

DEVILED DANNY

FRANKIE FRITTATA

FUZZY FLORENTINE

PEPE RANCHEROS

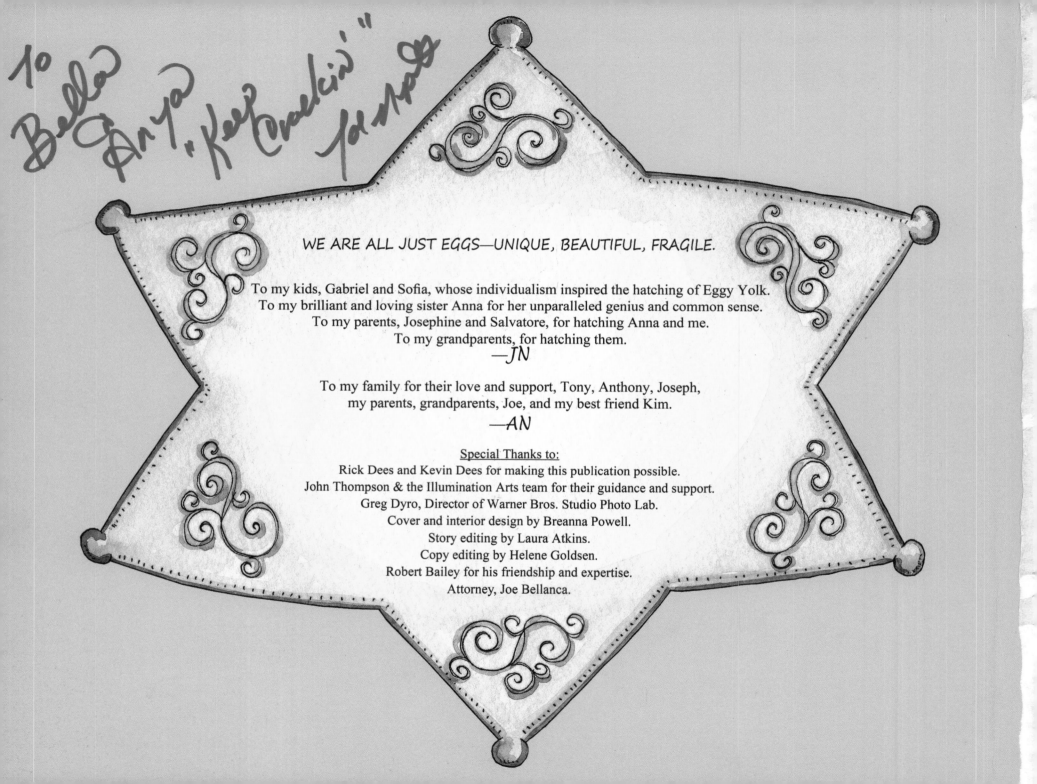

WE ARE ALL JUST EGGS—UNIQUE, BEAUTIFUL, FRAGILE.

To my kids, Gabriel and Sofia, whose individualism inspired the hatching of Eggy Yolk.
To my brilliant and loving sister Anna for her unparalleled genius and common sense.
To my parents, Josephine and Salvatore, for hatching Anna and me.
To my grandparents, for hatching them.
—JN

To my family for their love and support, Tony, Anthony, Joseph,
my parents, grandparents, Joe, and my best friend Kim.
—AN

Special Thanks to:
Rick Dees and Kevin Dees for making this publication possible.
John Thompson & the Illumination Arts team for their guidance and support.
Greg Dyro, Director of Warner Bros. Studio Photo Lab.
Cover and interior design by Breanna Powell.
Story editing by Laura Atkins.
Copy editing by Helene Goldsen.
Robert Bailey for his friendship and expertise.
Attorney, Joe Bellanca.

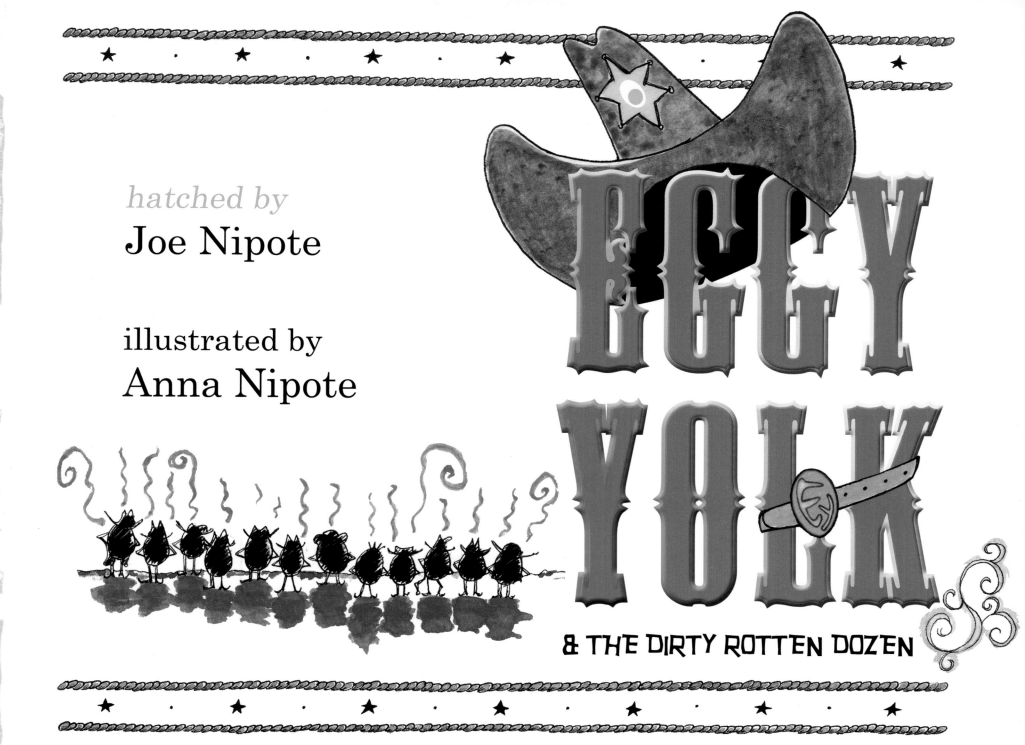

hatched by
Joe Nipote

illustrated by
Anna Nipote

EGGY YOLK

& THE DIRTY ROTTEN DOZEN

It was a bright sunny-side-up morning in Eggville, and the happy oval TOWNSYOLK were sizzling with EGGCITEMENT, because their new sheriff had just arrived. His name was Eggy Yolk.

However, trouble was also brewing on this special day, and what happened next is a true American YOLKTALE...

Just outside of town, the notorious Dirty Rotten Dozen was terrorizing one of the local YOLKELS.

The Dirty Rotten Dozen was the meanest—smelliest—rottenest batch of DESPEREGGOS, and anyone who dared to stand in their way was EGGSTERMINATED.

After they tossed Farmer Gregg, the grubby gang sent him into town with a message for the new sheriff.

"**I**t was the Dirty Rotten Dozen," moaned Farmer Gregg.

Everyone gasped at the mere mention of that name.

"They flipped me like a western omelet and forced me to sign over the deed to my farm. Then they took Pegg and Megg," he sobbed.

Doc Shellby whispered to Eggy, "I've got to patch his crack right now or he'll be nothing but an empty shell."

"Don't you run out on me," Eggy said. "We'll get your family and your farm back."

"Wait!" cried Farmer Gregg. "They'll be here by high noon to take over Eggville."

Noon was only an hour away, and Eggy needed help. He asked for deputies, but Mayor Albumin and the others just made up lame **EGGSCUSES** and scrambled inside.

Right on time, the Dirty Rotten Dozen **EGGSPLODED** into Eggville. Leading the super stinky bunch was their boss, Hardboiled Harry—A REAL BAD EGG.

Riding behind him and his hostages were the rest of the Dirty Rotten Dozen...

"That's far enough Hardboiled," Eggy called out in a nasally voice. You and your gang are under arrest for EGGTOSSING, EGGSTORTION, EGGNAPPING, and stinking up the place."

"Chicken feathers! I'm the new sheriff now," Hardboiled belched. "So hand over your badge and beat it!"

"I took an oath to protect and serve the citizens of Eggville," Eggy fired back.

"You've got raw courage. I like that." Hardboiled smirked. "Most TOWNSYOLK walk on eggshells around me, but you're different. So OM-E-LET you save your shell if—you join my gang."

"I wasn't hatched yesterday," Eggy said boldly. "Only a fool would trust a rotten egg."

"Then you and the rest of these yella-bellies will end up cooked!" Hardboiled yelled. "Benedict, whip him into hollandaise sauce."

Benedict Benny was an expert marksman who never refused a bet, and Eggy knew it—so he quickly filled the biggest balloon with extra helium and said, "I heard you were the best, but I'll betcha can't hit this ring."

Benny couldn't help himself and took the bet.

"*QUICHE* him bye-bye," Eggy chuckled.

Hardboiled was STEWING mad. "Pound him into an hors d'oeuvre," he commanded Pepe Rancheros.

Pepe drew his shiny ball-peen hammers and rushed toward Eggy.

"Yummy!"

Eggy waited til he saw
the whites of Pepe's eyes
to reach for his secret weapon.

The sprinting stallion saw
the juicy treat and slammed on his brakes. Next,
Eggy drew his slingshot and popped Benny's balloon.

"That's what I call egg-drop soup," he laughed.

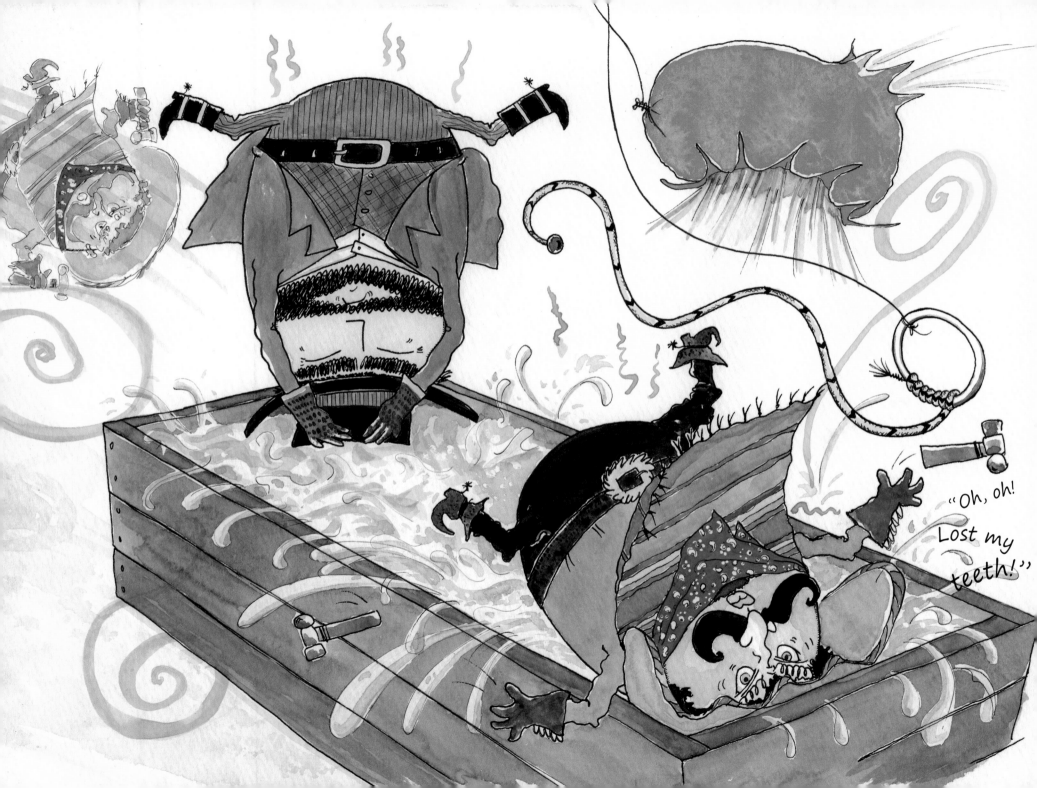

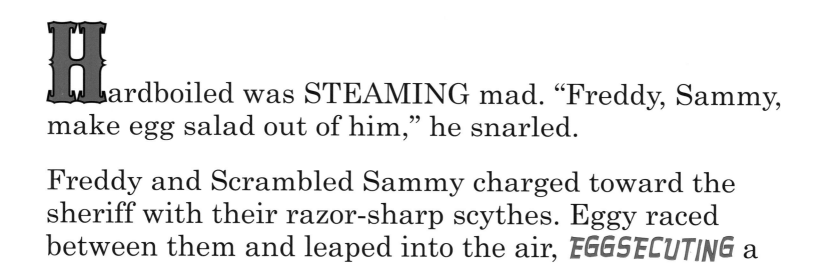

Hardboiled was STEAMING mad. "Freddy, Sammy, make egg salad out of him," he snarled.

Freddy and Scrambled Sammy charged toward the sheriff with their razor-sharp scythes. Eggy raced between them and leaped into the air, EGGSECUTING a perfect somersault as they swung and missed…him.

"That's two eggs over easy," Eggy giggled.

Hardboiled was now BOILING mad. He switched his patch over to his left eye and bellowed, "The rest of ya! BREAK THAT EGGHEAD!"

But it was too late. The timid TOWNSYOLK emerged from their hiding places and took the sulfuric scoundrels by surprise.

Eggy's EGGSTRAORDINARY acts of courage had finally inspired them to stand up to the rotten eggs.

The Dirty Rotten Dozen were then whisked away to prison, where they would surely fry.

That evening, Mayor Albumin called a special Town Hall meeting and proposed that the town's name be changed to...

Everyone was so grateful to Eggy for saving Eggville—and helping them rediscover their *INTEGGRITY*—they all voted with a resounding YES.

Even Farmer Gregg was there hoping to thank Eggy, but he was already wobbling home, singing and strumming his *YOLKELELE*. Eggy didn't care much for all the hoopla—he figured he was just doing his job. The *TOWNSYOLK* figured he was just *EGGSHAUSTED*.

"To our new sheriff, Eggy Yolk," the mayor proclaimed. "A MIGHTY GOOD EGG!"

THE BALLAD OF EGGY YOLK

HE'S THE STUFF OMELETS ARE MADE OF

BUT NOTHIN' 'BOUT HIM'S CHEESY

IF HE SCRAMBLES WITH A ROTTEN EGG

HE'LL FLIP HIM OVER EASY

HE'S NOT A YELLA-BELLY

OR A FANCY HORS D'OEUVRE

HE'S JUST A GOOD EGG

WHO TOOK AN OATH TO SERVE

EGGY YOLK!

"SEE YA, PARTNER"

3601 West Olive Avenue Suite #675
Burbank, CA 91505
Eggy@EggyYolk.com • EggyYolk.com

ISBN 9780-9855417-6-7

First printing, 2014
Published in the United States of America
Printed by Shanghai Chenxi Printing Co., Ltd.

Designers: Illumination Arts, Bellevue, WA
with Breanna Powell Design, Maple Valley, WA

WANTED
THE DIRTY ROTTEN DOZEN
COOKED OR ALIVE

HARDBOILED HARRY

CODDLED CORRIGAN

FRIED FREDDY

SCRAMBLED SAMMY

PICKLED PAULIE

STUFFED STUEY